Hello Kitty

and friends

The Dance Camp

·A HELLO KITTY ADVENTURE·

Hello Kitty
and friends

The Dance Camp
·A HELLO KITTY ADVENTURE·

HarperCollins *Children's Books*

MEET

Hello Kitty

and friends

Hello Kitty

Mimmy

Tammy

Mama

Papa

Grandpa

Grandma

Fifi

Dear Daniel

With special thanks to
Linda Chapman and Michelle Misra

First published in Great Britain by HarperCollins Children's Books in 2015

www.harpercollins.co.uk
1 3 5 7 9 10 8 6 4 2
ISBN: 978-0-00-754070-9

Printed and bound in England by Clays Ltd, St Ives plc.

FSC
www.fsc.org   FSC C007454

FSC™ is a non-profit international organisation established to promote
the responsible management of the world's forests. Products carrying the
FSC label are independently certified to assure consumers that they come
from forests that are managed to meet the social, economic and
ecological needs of present and future generations,
and other controlled sources.

Find out more about HarperCollins and the environment at
www.harpercollins.co.uk/green

Contents

Contents

Dance Camp!

Hello Kitty fastened the pink bow in her
hair and then twirled in front of her bedroom
mirror. She was really excited! It was the first
day of holidays and she was about to go on a
week-long dance and music camp. Her three

best friends were going to be there too – Dear
Daniel, Fifi and Tammy. ***Together*** they made
up the Friendship Club. They had meetings
where they baked and made things, had
sleepovers and went on outings. They also liked
to make up rules about friendship, things like:

*Good friends make
hard things easy to do.*

Just then, Hello Kitty's bedroom door

opened and her twin sister Mimmy looked in.

Mimmy had a blue bow in her hair; she always

wore her bow on the right and Hello Kitty

always wore her bow on the left so that people

could tell them apart. It was time to go to camp.

They didn't want to be late on their first day!

Hello Kitty *and friends*

Hello Kitty grabbed her bag and ran downstairs with Mimmy. Papa was holding the car keys and heading out the door as Mama came into the hall, carrying a couple of full rubbish bags.

What was she doing, asked Hello Kitty? Mama **smiled** and explained that she had decided to spend the day having

a good sort out of their old toys – the ones they used to play with. Some were broken and needed to be thrown away, and others could be given to charity.

Mimmy looked a bit worried. Mama wouldn't get rid any of the toys they still played with, would she?

Mama promised she wouldn't throw any toys away without checking with Mimmy and Hello Kitty first. All she was going to do that day was sort them out, and then when the girls came home they could *decide* which toys they would like to give away. It was such a shame to have toys in the house that they never played with, she said – it would be much better for them to be given to younger children who would really enjoy them.

Hello Kitty and Mimmy looked at Mama and nodded. It would be lovely to think of their old toys making other children **happy!** But it was time to go; they gave Mama a quick hug and raced out to get into the car.

The girls chattered non-stop on the way to camp. What was it going to be like? Mimmy loved music and wanted to play her flute all

week while Hello Kitty wanted to spend the week dancing. The camp had lots of different classes to choose from. They couldn't wait to find out more!

As Papa drove into the car park,

Hello Kitty saw Dear Daniel, Fifi and Tammy already there with their parents. They all smiled and waved when they saw her, and after Papa parked the car Hello Kitty **jumped** out and ran over to them. Were they as excited about camp as she was? Of course they were!

A bell rang. It was time for the camp to start!

All the students gathered together in a big hall. The lady in **charge** of the camp stood on the stage and told them a bit about it. She explained that there would be all sorts of dance and music sessions running every morning and afternoon. Hello Kitty listened hard as she listed the different dance classes there would be...

Ballet

Tap

Jazz

Pop

There would be all sorts of music classes too, and you could choose whichever ones you wanted! Hello Kitty *really* wanted to do ballet. She shut her eyes, imagining herself in a pink tutu and ballet shoes, pirouetting around and leaping lightly into the air. She glanced at her friends. They all looked like they were lost in happy daydreams too.

The lady was still talking. Hello Kitty heard the words '*music and dance display*' and jerked to attention, as the lady was saying something very interesting! At the end of the week there would be a music and dance contest – students could enter in groups and do either a short dance or play a short piece of music together.

There would even be a prize for the **best** dance group and the **best** music group! Hello Kitty felt a tingle of excitement as she imagined ballet dancing on a stage with her friends. The Friendship Club HAD to enter!

WINNER

1

As the talk ended, Fifi and Tammy were whispering excitedly to each other and Dear Daniel **grinned** at her. Hello Kitty grinned back at him. She knew they were all thinking the same as her! They had ten minutes to check the schedule, decide which classes they wanted to do that morning and sign up for them.

As the lady stepped off the stage, the Friendship Club gathered together and started to talk at once. Tammy **burst** out that she was sure she could think up a tap dance display

for them all, but Fifi exclaimed **loudly**

that jazz sounded so fun! She was sure they

would all enjoy it and they could do a brilliant

routine. Dear Daniel was talking too – but

about the pop classes. Hello Kitty was surprised.

Didn't the others want to do ballet then, like

she did?

Fifi looked surprised.

No, ballet would be

boring. She wanted

to do jazz where you

got to do cartwheels

and stuff! Surely they all wanted to do that too?

The others shook their heads. Dear Daniel

said he had always wanted to learn to body

pop and Tammy put in that she was *really*

looking forward to learning to tap dance.

Oh dear! They had all been daydreaming

about dancing but they had been daydreaming

about different dance classes! How was this

going to work out?

The lady at the front clapped her hands.

Could everyone sign up for the classes they

wanted to do that day please? The Friendship

Club looked at each other. Whatever were they

going to do **now?**

Ballet Class

Hello Kitty looked round at her friends.

Maybe they should just go to different classes so

that they could all learn the dances they actually

wanted to do? The others all shook their heads.

They were the Friendship Club! They should

definitely go to classes together and do the display as a group at the end of the week. They didn't want to split up! They would have to choose one class to go to… But how were they going to do that?

Fifi's eyes lit up with an idea. Why didn't they all choose a different class for them to try out together, just for the first day, and then they could have a vote at the end as to which one to keep doing? Maybe then they would find out that they all liked the same class after all.

Hello Kitty and the others nodded. That sounded like a super plan! So they went to the board and signed up for the classes. First

they would do ballet, then jazz, and after lunch
they would go to tap and pop. It was going to
be a VERY busy day!

As she waited for her friends to sign the list,
Hello Kitty saw Mimmy signing up for music
classes with her friend, Alice, and three other
girls who Mimmy and Alice **played** with in
the junior band. Hello Kitty went over to say

hello, and Mimmy introduced
her to the others. There was
Lily who played the trumpet,
Katie who played the violin
and Sandy
who played
the keyboards. Hello Kitty
already knew Alice of
course!

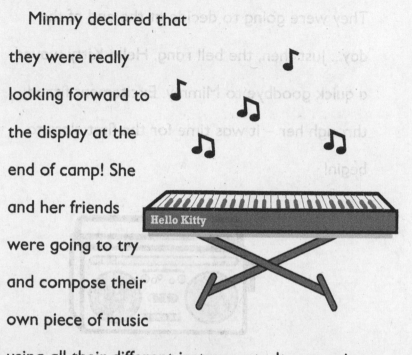

Mimmy declared that they were really looking forward to the display at the end of camp! She and her friends were going to try and compose their own piece of music using all their different instruments. It was going to be so much **fun!** What about Hello Kitty?

Hello Kitty explained that she and her friends were going to do a dance display, but they still didn't know what type of dance they would do.

They were going to decide at the end of the

day... Just then, the bell rang. Hello Kitty waved

a quick goodbye to Mimmy. Excitement fizzed

through her – it was time for the first class to

begin!

The beautiful soft music played on the CD

player, echoing around the dance studio. Hello

Kitty held on to the ballet barre and gracefully

bent and straightened her legs, copying the

teacher's arm and feet positions. She lifted her chin and pointed her toes as well as she could. The teacher smiled at her. Hello Kitty was a *natural!*

Hello Kitty and friends

Hello Kitty blushed with pride. But then she looked in the mirror on the wall and caught sight of her friends. **Oh dear!** They definitely didn't look like they were having such a good time. Dear Daniel was pulling a face as he tried to turn his feet out into the first position. Tammy was out of time with everyone else, and Fifi was bored and springing up and down on the spot instead of doing the movements the teacher wanted.

Hello Kitty's heart sank. She had been hoping her friends would decide they really liked ballet, but it wasn't looking likely. Still, she comforted herself, it was only the first half hour of the class…

After they had done their exercises, the teacher put some new music on and asked them to dance round the room pretending that they were autumn leaves, *swirling* and *twirling* through the air and falling to the ground.

Hello Kitty ran gracefully around, spinning and turning, but Dear Daniel looked embarrassed and didn't go faster than a walk.

Tammy's arms were stiff and Fifi jumped around so much, she looked more like a bouncing ball than a gently falling leaf!

Hello Kitty sighed. The ballet class wasn't turning out as she had hoped at all. After the class, when they were putting their trainers back on, some of the other girls in the class started talking to Hello Kitty. They were really nice, and they all loved ballet too. They were surprised when they heard she wasn't

coming back after the break but was going to a

different class instead – especially when she was

so good at ballet! Hello Kitty wished she could

come back, but it was time for jazz class and

she had promised to go.

She glanced round and saw Fifi, Tammy

and Dear Daniel waiting by the door for her.

Whoops! She'd better go!

She called goodbye to the

girls and jumped up to join

her friends.

3

Hard Choices

Fifi was super-excited about going to the

jazz class! She *skipped* and jumped all the

way there. The teacher was young and fun and

made them do a very fast, bouncy warm-up.

Dear Daniel and Tammy couldn't keep up at all.

Hello Kitty was having fun and liked the routine the teacher taught them but Dear Daniel couldn't do the cartwheels and Tammy was totally *puffed* out. At the end they both declared that neither of them ever wanted to go to a jazz class again! So that was another class they couldn't do as a group.

Still, maybe the pop or tap classes would be a hit with all of them that afternoon?

They weren't. Fifi didn't like the tap dancing

because she couldn't **spring** and jump, and none

of them apart from Dear Daniel liked the pop

class where they had to learn to dance like

robots. Hello Kitty wanted to *swirl* and *twirl*

and point her toes, not be stiff like a robot!

PREMIÈRE
ÉTOILE
Hello Kitty

Hello Kitty and friends

By the end of the day they still didn't know what type of dance they were they going to learn for the rest of the week. **Oh dear**.

When Mama came to pick up Hello Kitty and Mimmy, Hello Kitty asked her if the others could come home for tea. They needed to have a Friendship Club meeting so they could vote on what dance class to do.

🎵 🎵 🎵 The Dance Camp

Mama smiled; of course they could all come back – but she warned Hello Kitty that the kitchen was a mess! She was still sorting out all their old toys. The Friendship Club would have to have a picnic tea on a rug in the lounge because there was no room at the table. Hello Kitty smiled. That sounded *fun!*

When they got back, they found the kitchen table was *covered* with toys. There were broken toys in one pile, baby toys like rattles and building blocks in another pile and then a third pile — the biggest — which was all the toys Mama wanted Hello Kitty and Mimmy to look at before she gave them to the charity shop.

Hello Kitty and Mimmy started looking

through the pile. Hello Kitty saw her old stuffed

clown and pulled him out.

She'd loved playing with

him when she was

little, making him

tumble around

and do cartwheels.

Mimmy picked

up her old wind-up

penguin and wound the

little plastic key. When she

let him go, he *spun* round in a funny dance,

tapping his feet. She couldn't give him away!

Or the musical box with the spinning

ballerina, or Hello Kitty's collection of plastic

fairies, or the funny tin robot...

Mama **smiled** and shook her head at them.

They couldn't keep *everything!* There wasn't

room in the house for all their

old toys and they could make

some little children very

happy. But they could

decide later when their

friends had gone. She shooed them out into the

lounge and told them she would bring some

food through soon.

Mimmy went off to her room to practise her

flute and The Friendship Club sat down in a

circle. So... *which* dance

class were they going

to do? Hello Kitty

announced that they

should have a vote.

How many people

wanted to do ballet?

Hello Kitty was the only

one who put up her hand.

OK, how many people wanted to do jazz? Fifi put up her hand.

And tap dancing? Tammy's hand shot in the air.

And with pop, it was Dear Daniel's turn to raise his hand. **Oh no!** They hadn't got any further with deciding at all.

And they really had to if they were going to start working out a dance display for the end of the week. What were they going to do?

Dear Daniel thought for a minute, and suggested that since they couldn't decide, they should put the name of the *different* dances into a hat and pick one out. The others agreed it was the best solution. So Hello Kitty found one of Papa's hats, wrote ballet, tap, jazz and pop on to **four** bits of paper and then asked Mama to come in and pull one out.

They all waited eagerly as she reached into the hat. What dance were they going to be learning?

Hello Kitty and friends

Mama picked out a piece of paper and
unfolded it. It said…. BALLET!

Ballet

Hello Kitty gave a **gasp** of delight but then she heard her friends all sigh and her happiness faded straightaway. She didn't want her friends to have to go to dance classes they wouldn't enjoy! She took a deep breath, and told them they should pick another dance out of the hat instead.

But the others shook their heads! Dear Daniel said they'd had an agreement and they would do ballet; it was fairer that way. The others nodded. They would just have to make the best of it. They

Hello Kitty and friends

would go to the ballet classes and work out a ballet display. Hello Kitty smiled at her friends. She was so **lucky** to have them!

Mama squeezed her shoulder and said that
sounded like a good idea, but now the picnic
was ready, so they could talk about it more in
a minute. Everyone **jumped**
up to help her bring it
into the lounge. Mama
had made some
sandwiches and
there were little
sweet tomatoes,
chunks of cucumber
and mini sausages
too. **Yummy!**

Mimmy came down to join them and they

had a lovely picnic tea, **_finishing_** off all

the sandwiches before having some chocolate

brownies for pudding. No one said anything

more about learning ballet but Hello Kitty still

felt **unhappy**. She didn't want her friends to

have to go to a dance class that they didn't

want to do.

After everyone else had gone home, she and

Mimmy sorted through the toys. They put the

broken ones into a rubbish bag and the baby

toys into a cardboard box before they started

sorting through the other toys. It was very hard to give them away, but they knew Mama was *right!* It was silly keeping things if they never played with them. They cleaned the toys up with warm water and soap and then packed them all away into another box, ready to go to the charity shop when Mama next went into town.

Mama came in and kissed them both. Now they would have **lots** of space in their bedrooms for new toys when Christmas came, and they should feel very happy knowing that they would be making other children **happy** too!

Hello Kitty and Mimmy smiled at each other. Mama was right.

Hello Kitty *and friends*

Later that night, Hello Kitty went upstairs and got ready for bed. Tomorrow she would be doing ballet classes with the others all day. She wished she felt more **excited** at the thought, but it was hard to be excited when she knew her friends wouldn't enjoy it!

She thought about the display at the end of
the week. Maybe they could do a dance from
Swan Lake? But no. She just *couldn't* see
her friends pretending to be beautiful, dreamy
swans when they weren't happy. So what sort of
ballet dance could she imagine them all doing?

She sighed. She really didn't know at all!

4

Mimmy's Bright Idea

The next morning when Hello Kitty went
to the ballet studio, the other girls in the class
were waiting in the corridor practising their
steps. They were **very** pleased to see Hello
Kitty again and waved as soon as they saw her.

She ran over and joined in with them. But when

she looked round, she saw Dear Daniel, Fifi

and Tammy sitting *quietly* on a bench. Hello

Kitty felt very bad for them. She excused herself

from her new friends and went to sit with

the Friendship Club. *Oh*, how she wished her

friends liked ballet more!

Tammy gave her a gentle push and whispered that Hello Kitty **really** didn't have to sit with them; she could go and practise if she wanted to. But Hello Kitty shook her head. She would feel like she was abandoning the Friendship Club.

🎵 The Dance Camp

Their teacher opened the doors and they all
piled into the studio. The class was very similar
to the day before – it *started* with exercises
at the barre and then in the centre of the room.

Hello Kitty *and friends*

Hello Kitty found it hard to enjoy herself. Her friends tried hard to look as if they were enjoying it but she could tell they weren't *really* having fun.

As soon as the class was over, they all hurried off to the middle of camp for their

 break. Hello Kitty took her time, chatting with the other girls about their favourite ballets and the classes they went to normally. Finally she

headed over to **find** the rest of the Friendship

Club. Where were they? What were they doing?

She saw that Dear Daniel was playing

football with some of the boys who had

been in the pop class the day before.

TAP

TAP

TAP

TAP

Tammy was with the tap dancers who were

showing her some **moves** they had learnt

that morning in class and Fifi was with the jazz

students listening to some music. They were all

smiling and laughing. Hello Kitty felt as if she

had a **knot** in her tummy. They looked much

happier than they had in the ballet class!

She sat down by herself, wishing she knew
what to do. Someone called her name and
she looked round. It was Mimmy and Alice!
Mimmy asked her if she was all
right, and Hello Kitty

shook her head.

She explained
about the dance
classes and
the rest of the
Friendship Club
having to do
ballet when they
didn't like it.

Mimmy frowned. Why couldn't Hello Kitty and her friends just go to **different** dance classes if they all liked doing different kinds of dance?

Hello Kitty was puzzled. They were friends – they wanted to be together.

Mimmy pointed out that they could still be friends and do different classes. Alice nodded. Their friends from band all played different instruments so they were in different classes, but they saw each other at break and lunch. It didn't mean they weren't friends.

And, Alice added, being in different classes meant they had the *fun* of making new friends!

Hello Kitty thought of the friendly girls in her ballet class. She **would** really like to get to know them better. Dear Daniel, Fifi and Tammy would always be her best ever friends but that didn't mean she couldn't have other friends.

But wait a minute, she put in – what about the dance display? They needed to be doing the same sort of dance to go in it together!

Mimmy **shrugged**. She and Alice and their other friends were thinking up a musical piece that used all their different instruments. Couldn't Hello Kitty and the rest of the Friendship Club do something similar? They could put all the different types of dance together; it would be ***fantastic!*** Mimmy smiled.

Hello Kitty felt as if a light bulb had gone on over her head. That was a brilliant idea! She had to talk to the others!

Hello Kitty gathered the Friendship Club together and told them what Mimmy and Alice had said. They could go to *different* dance classes, and do something that used all the different styles for their display! They would still be best friends, but they would be **happier** because they would all be doing the type of dance they liked best, and they could make new friends too.

Everyone started talking at once. It was a great idea!

Dear Daniel put in that they would need to work really hard to come up with a display that used all the different kinds of *dance*. They might not have enough time...

They would if they had a Friendship Club meeting every day after camp, Fifi pointed out. They could go to each other's houses every night and practise the routine! It could be the *best* dance ever if they worked really hard!

Hello Kitty nodded eagerly. Why didn't everyone come round to her house that evening and they could get started then… Did they all want to? Her friends all grinned. **Of course** they did!

They all ran to the board and changed their names to the different classes, and waved **goodbye** until lunchtime as they ran off to their classes.

Ballet

Hello Kitty

~~Dear Daniel~~

~~Fifi~~

~~Tammy~~

Hello Kitty *and friends*

Hello Kitty really enjoyed her ballet class now she wasn't worried about whether her friends were having a good time too. She learnt how to do jumps and how to stand **gracefully** on one leg with the other out behind her. She couldn't wait to show the others when classes finished!

They had dance steps to show her too. Fifi showed them the routine she was learning with three cartwheels in it, Dear Daniel *showed* them a few of his new robotic moves and Tammy showed them some tap dancing steps she'd learned. They all had so much to talk about now that they were in different classes and they even had new friends to introduce everyone to.

But what could they do for the display? After camp, they went back to Hello Kitty's house to try and **decide**. They needed a dance that they could all do. They sat in the kitchen around the table and ate chocolate chip cookies as they talked about it.

Fifi bounced up and down and called out that she

thought that it would be good if their dance had

a story! Maybe they could do a woodland dance

and all be animals. She could be a lively squirrel

and Hello Kitty could be an elegant deer!

But what about Dear Daniel and Tammy?

None of them could think of any woodland

animals that moved like robots

or tap danced!

They thought again. Hello Kitty drummed her fingers on the edge of the box with *all* the toys in it as she thought hard. What dance could they do?

She looked at the toy box... and that was it! What about a dance about toys?

As the others carried on talking she took the lid off the box and looked at the toys inside. It just **might** work. Dear Daniel could be a toy robot.

Fifi could be a tumbling, cartwheeling toy clown, Tammy could be a wind-up, tap dancing penguin. And as for Hello Kitty herself? Maybe

she could be a teddy bear?
No, she wanted to be
something pretty and
graceful, something like
a *fairy*...

That was it! The perfect story suddenly
popped into Hello Kitty's head. She could be
a fairy who brought the toys to life. She could
go twirling round the stage in
a fairy costume and ballet
shoes, tapping the others with
a wand so they could each do their own dance.
At the end they could all go back to sleep and
she would twirl away.

She gasped in delight. It would be perfect!

The others all looked at her as they heard

her gasp. What was it – did she have an idea,

they all wanted to know? Hello Kitty's eyes

glowed and she grinned as she looked at her

friends. Just **wait** until they heard her idea!

The Big Dance!

Fifi, Dear Daniel and Tammy all loved Hello Kitty's idea for the dance display. They could each do a dance that would suit them but the dances would all go together in a neat story! Fifi jumped up and tried out a few clown steps

The Dance Camp

and Dear Daniel started doing a robot dance as
Tammy started tapping away, with Hello Kitty
twirling around all of them. They were making
so much noise dancing and **giggling** that
Mama came in. Whatever was going on?

They all spoke at once to tell her Hello Kitty's idea. Mama thought it was **wonderful!** She would help them make costumes. She had some black and white material that would make a great penguin costume and some old curtains that she could sew into a clown costume. Hello Kitty could have a pretty tutu and wings and Dear Daniel's costume could be made out of cardboard boxes painted silver.

Hello Kitty got some paper. Soon they were all busy drawing their costumes and making lists of everything they would need. They agreed that they would all start *thinking* about their dances that night and then they could show the others the next day. Finally, they had a plan! And it was going to be super!

The Friendship Club had never worked as hard as they did that week. Every day they went to their dance classes and in the evenings they met up at each other's houses and practised their dances, *watching* and helping each other make them better.

Mama made their costumes. Each day their
dances got better and better. On Friday night
they had a *dress* rehearsal at Hello Kitty's
house where they tried on on their costumes
and put all the dances together. Mama and

Papa watched. They both clapped really hard at the end and said it was *really* good!

Hello Kitty went to bed that night feeling very excited. She didn't know if the Friendship Club would have the best dance but they'd had a lot of fun getting ready for it, and that was the main thing!

At lunchtime the next day, she and the rest of the Friendship Club were waiting at the side of the stage in their costumes. All the parents had arrived and were sitting in the hall, **watching** the different acts. The music students had all performed their pieces and most of the dance groups were done too. Mimmy and her friends had sounded really good and the Friendship Club had clapped loudly when they had finished. Now it was almost their turn on the stage!

They were the last group. Butterflies fluttered in Hello Kitty's tummy. She hoped everything was going to go well, and that she didn't trip up or forget her steps!

So far there had been lots of other dance groups, but none of them had done a **mixture** of dances. A group from Hello Kitty's ballet class had performed a scene from Swan Lake, a group from Fifi's class had danced to a pop song and there had been lots of other great dancing. They had all been good and the Friendship Club had clapped enthusiastically for all of them. But finally it was their turn!

The curtains shut and it was time for the Friendship Club to go on. All their new friends who were *watching* at the side of the stage gave them the thumbs up. Fifi, Dear Daniel and Tammy ran on, took their places and stood perfectly still. Hello Kitty waited at the side until the curtains opened and she heard the first notes of the fairy-like music that she had chosen. Then she took a **deep** breath, pointed her toes and danced into the light, her chin high, her back straight, and her wand outstretched.

She twirled gracefully around the others and then tapped Fifi with her wand. The music changed to a lively, bouncing beat. Hello Kitty danced to the side and waited as Fifi the clown sprang into life. She tumbled and cartwheeled around the

stage in perfect time to her music before flopping down on her tummy to watch as Hello Kitty danced over and touched Tammy. As the tap dancing music started, Tammy's head shot up and she was off, tap dancing from side to side, her tap

shoes making a smart tip-tapping noise with

every step she took. When she finished, Hello

Kitty twirled again, and it was Dear Daniel's

turn! His robot dance was **brilliant** – he really

did look just like a toy robot who

had just come to life.

At the end, Hello Kitty

touched each of them with

her wand again and they

pretended to fall back

to sleep. Hello Kitty

did one final twirl,

waved her wand at the

audience and danced off the side of the stage.

Everything was quiet for a moment, and then the audience **exploded** into claps and cheers! Some people stood up they were so impressed. Hello Kitty and the others ran back on to take a bow. It was wonderful looking out at all the clapping, smiling people. Hello Kitty could see Mama in the audience beaming with delight, with Papa cheering beside her.

They all ran off stage, grinning from ear to ear, to wait with the other students from the camp while the judges had a quick

talk. And then the announcement came – The

Friendship Club had WON!

They ran back on stage, where the head judge

said how **wonderful** it had been to see all the

different kinds of dancing put together. Hello

Kitty and her friends all blushed and smiled as the

audience clapped and the judge congratulated

them, before presenting them with a big silver

shield and a **massive** box of

chocolates! Hooray!

As the curtains closed, Hello Kitty and the rest

of the Friendship Club were surrounded by their

new friends. They opened the box of chocolates

and shared them out with everyone.

They all grinned and agreed that it had been the best holiday camp ever! Hello Kitty looked round at all the happy faces. She was so glad that she and the rest of the Friendship Club had decided to go to different dance classes in the end – they'd had so much more fun than they would have done if they'd all tried to stick together.

A new Friendship rule popped into her head:

Good Friends Can Be Different Because Their Friendship Still Stays The Same.

She smiled – she couldn't wait to tell the others!

But for now the camp teachers turned some disco music on, turned on the coloured lights and opened the curtains to the audience – it was time for everyone to have a *party* to celebrate the end of camp! Everyone ran on to the stage to dance to the music. Hello Kitty ran out to join them and was soon swirling and twirling with her friends, old and new, in the glittering, shining lights. Super!

The end

**Turn over the page for activities and
fun things that you can do with your
friends – just like Hello Kitty!**

Fairy Fun!

For the Friendship Club's big dance, Hello Kitty dresses as a magical fairy who brings toys to life. Follow the instructions here to make your very own fairy crown and wand, and see if you can make your own magic!

MAKE SURE YOU ASK MAMA OR PAPA TO HELP!

You will need:

PVA Glue (with a brush for spreading it)

Scissors

A stapler with staples

50 cm of white elastic

Gold or coloured glitter

A thick drinking straw (not a bendy one)

3 A4 pieces of white card

Pretty ribbons

A ruler or measuring tape

The Wand!

6 CM

What to do:

1. Copy or trace the template above on to your white card twice, and cut out the two stars.

2. Cover each star in a thin layer of glue, and sprinkle them with glitter until they're completely covered. Leave them to dry.

3. When your stars are dry, put one on each side of the end of the drinking straw with the glitter facing out. Staple through the middle of the two stars and the straw so they're all stuck together.

4. Tie the pretty ribbons on to the end of your straw, just underneath the star, so that the ends dangle.

Wave your wand and make some magic!

The Crown!

What to do:

1. Measure how much white elastic you will need to go around your head, making sure to leave a bit extra so you can tie the ends together in a knot to make it into a band.

2. Measure how many stars you will need to cover your band in them – each star is 6cm across. You might need a grown-up's help to figure this out!

3. Copy or trace the star template on to your white card for how many stars you need, and cut each one out carefully.

4. Cover each star in a thin layer of glue, and sprinkle them with glitter until they're completely covered. Leave them to dry.

5. While your stars are drying, tie the ends of your elastic together so that it makes a ring that will fit around your head.

6. Staple the stars through the middle on to your elastic band, making sure they are all spaced evenly apart and the same way up.

Now Hello Kitty says put on your pretty fairy crown, wave your magic wand, and dance dance dance!

Turn the page for a sneak peek at

and friends'

next adventure...

The Camping Trip

Hello Kitty stood back from her bed and looked at her packing – her clothes were in neat rows, her hair bows were set out, her shoes were in a line and her pink flowery sleeping bag was all rolled up. She hadn't forgotten anything, had she? Just then, her twin sister Mimmy bounced into the room with a backpack. Mimmy laughed and pointed out that Hello Kitty might have put out all of the things that she wanted to take camping but hadn't she forgotten the most important things?

What sort of things? Hello Kitty looked at everything she had laid out.

Mimmy started pulling things out of her backpack and putting them on the bed next to Hello Kitty's things. She had:

A water bottle

Some Binoculars

A tube of sunscreen

A Torch

Hello Kitty grinned. Mimmy was right! They

did need to take things like that, but she was having lots of fun packing things to wear. After all, she wanted to look nice when they got there!

At that moment, Mama White came in and gasped when she saw what Hello Kitty was planning on taking. They were going away for a weekend, not a whole month! She smiled and said that Hello Kitty would need to put some of it back – or there wouldn't be any room in the tent for the Friendship Club!

Hello Kitty giggled and thought about her friends in the Friendship Club – Dear Daniel, Fifi and Tammy. Usually the four of them met after school and in the holidays to do all sorts of fun things like arts and crafts, baking and having sleepovers, but this weekend Hello Kitty's parents were taking them camping. Mama and Papa were going to be in one tent and Hello Kitty and the Friendship Club would be in the one next door, as well as Mimmy and her friend Alice. It was going to be so much fun!

Find out what happens next in...

Coming soon!

Hello Kitty and friends

The Camping Trip
·A HELLO KITTY ADVENTURE·

Coming soon!

The Camping Trip
·A HELLO KITTY ADVENTURE·

Collect all of the Hello Kitty and Friends Stories!

The Cupcake Mystery
·A HELLO KITTY ADVENTURE·

The Dance Camp
·A HELLO KITTY ADVENTURE·

The Big Race

The Makeover Party
·A HELLO KITTY ADVENTURE·

The Animal Adventure
·A HELLO KITTY ADVENTURE·

The Halloween Parade
·A HELLO KITTY ADVENTURE·

The Magazine Mix-Up
·A HELLO KITTY ADVENTURE·

The TV Star
·A HELLO KITTY ADVENTURE·

The Friendship Club

The School Trip

The Summer Fair

The Pop Princess

The Wedding Day

The Beach Holiday

The Treasure Hunt

The Talent Show

The Christmas Present
TWO SPECIAL CHRISTMAS STORIES

Christmas Special:
Two Stories in One!